# FRANK
## THE NEWPORT FOX

# F.JOHN MCLAUGHLIN
## ILLUSTRATED BY GORDON D'ARCY

AuthorHouse™
1663 Liberty Drive
Bloomington, IN 47403
www.authorhouse.com
Phone: 833-262-8899

Because of the dynamic nature of the Internet, any web addresses or links contained in this book may have changed
since publication and may no longer be valid. The views expressed in this work are solely those of the author and do
not necessarily reflect the views of the publisher, and the publisher hereby disclaims any responsibility for them.

Any people depicted in stock imagery provided by Getty Images are models,
and such images are being used for illustrative purposes only.
Certain stock imagery © Getty Images.

This book is printed on acid-free paper.

ISBN: 978-1-6655-4433-7 (sc)
ISBN: 978-1-6655-4434-4 (hc)
ISBN: 978-1-6655-4432-0 (e)

Library of Congress Control Number: 2021923238

Print information available on the last page.

Published by AuthorHouse  11/15/2021

authorHOUSE

# CONTENTS

To My Granddaughter
Annabelle Marlette McLaughlin

Acknowledgments:   Rosemarie Boyd;Anne Jackson, "Words are My Work"; Elizabeth McLaughlin, and John Ganem for their help in bringing this tale to life.

# CHAPTER ONE

# The Arrival of the French

In 1780, King Louis XVI of France sent General Jean-Baptiste Rochambeau with six thousand soldiers and sixteen foxes to Newport, Rhode Island. This army was to support General George Washington in his revolution against King George III of England. King Louis had imagined that his army would enjoy hunting in the New World; hence his gift of eight dog foxes and eight vixen.

The first day out into the North Atlantic, the foxes escaped their pens and disappeared into the hold of the transport ship. They reappeared on deck shortly afterwards with large dead rats clenched in their teeth and deposited their prey at the feet of General Rochambeau. In a flash, he decided that the foxes would be far more valuable as hunters on board the ship than being hunted in America. He announced that the foxes should be granted free range of the ship provided that they rid the holds of vermin. The foxes hunted at night and dozed in the sunshine on the deck during the day. The voyage lasted three months. The foxes quickly became domesticated. They lined up every morning in the ship's galley for their daily rations from the chef. They were spoiled by the entire crew.

When they disembarked in Newport, General Rochambeau established a camp for his army in the orchards along BellevueAvenue. The foxes continued to keep the vermin under control. Five months later Rochambeau marched south with his army to join General Washington's army, and together they defeated General Cornwallis at the battle of Yorktown and won the war.

When the French army left Newport, the foxes were given their freedom. They went feral. They merged with the local population of foxes on Aquidneck Island, an island in Narragansett Bay, Rhode Island. The arrival of these sophisticated, cosmopolitan, suave, epicurean foxes transformed the rustic fox population.

# CHAPTER TWO

# Frank the Newport Fox

Frank lived with his vixen, Terry, and 3 cubs, Red, Rowan, and Johnny, in a luxurious den at the bottom of a garden on BellevueAvenue in Newport.

The den had been built during the golden age after the Civil War, when millionaires were coming to Newport to build their summer "cottages" (mansions). While the mansions were being built, Frank's grandfather, Ted, was busy building his den in a disused compost heap at the bottom of one of the mansion's gardens. He only used the finest construction materials that he could borrow. He dug an oblique main entrance that opened up into a large family room. The roof was supported by wooden columns. He laid down a mahogany floor and laid fine cherry planks on two wine crates to make a dining room table. Ted fashioned a chimney out of a discarded drain pipe. The pipe was hidden by a tangle of grapevine. Off the family room he dug a root cellar for storing fruits and vegetables for the winter months. Over the years, a main bedroom and a children's room with bunk beds had been constructed. Frank felt that it was by far the most comfortable den on Aquidneck Island.

The foxes loved living in the center of Newport at the junction of VanderbiltAvenue and Spring Street. It was an easy scramble from their den up the apple tree, over the brick wall and down to the restaurants on Thames Street. Foxes are nocturnal. They are able to sleep all day and go out on the town only at two o'clock in the morning. The restaurants are busy putting out their bins of leftover food. The cubs had developed a technique of quietly raising the lids of the bins to choose their dinner. One night it would be a steak restaurant, another night a seafood or a pizza restaurant. Once they had found enough food, they stealthily carried it back to their den. Red was the most accurate at tossing food. When they returned to their garden wall, Rowan climbed to the top, Johnny climbed down into the garden, and they formed a relay: Red tossed their dinner up to Rowan, Rowan dropped it down to Johnny, and Frank and Terry carried the food into the den and laid it out on the dining room table. They dined at dawn. All the foxes had to be home by then. Occasionally they got into street fights with foraging raccoons. However, the foxes always prevailed, having sharper teeth and being more agile than the slow, chubby raccoons. Foxes ate Roman style, lying on the ground beside their dining room table, feasting on their daily buffet. On this particular morning, Frank lay on his bed, mulling over the arrival of a new dangerous predator on Aquidneck Island. Coyotes! These were ferocious animals, four times the size of foxes. They hunted in packs of up to seven. They were ruthless, careless killers, often killing a whole garden of free range hens just for the fun of it. They were truly a threat to the survival of the foxes. Something had to be done about them. The random acts of violence on hens by the coyotes were being blamed on the foxes. The coyotes had to go.

While Frank was contemplating this dilemma, the garden gate swung open and an enormous truck started reversing into their garden! Frank and Terry peered out their front entrance. Workers were unloading a large mechanical digger. Two men were in the garden studying a large set of plans. Frank and Terry were horrified. Something was going to disturb their paradise. They decided then and there that they would have to evacuate their den that night and move to their summer den near Eaton's Beach until they figured out why the digger was in their garden. They let their cubs sleep that night. After a dinner of field mice and potatoes fresh from the garden, they explained to their children that they were relocating to their summer den. The cubs were ecstatic. They loved being beside the beach. By two o'clock in the morning, they were all packed and ready. Each fox had two plastic bags tied together over their shoulders. Frank and Terry packed leftover food and vegetables from their root cellar. The cubs packed their favorite toys and pillows. They set off Indian file down Memorial Drive to their summer den. It was in the rushes around Eaton's Pond, across to road from the Carousel and Eaton's Beach. They found that two brave rabbits had moved into their den, a fatal mistake. Frank knew that he didn't have to worry about dinner anymore.

The exhausted foxes collapsed into a deep sleep. The following night, Frank went to investigate what the digger was doing in his garden. As he peered over the wall he was shocked to see that the compost heap and his ancestral home were obliterated. Instead there was a deep rectangular hole in the ground. The property owners were installing an in-ground swimming pool. Their ancestral fox den, the finest in Newport, was gone forever.

## CHAPTER THREE

# Swept Away

Frank slunk back to their beach den to relate his sad news. He was surprised to find his vixen, Terry, in floods of tears when he crept quietly back into the den. He was puzzled. How could she possibly have found out about the catastrophe? When he was able to calm her down and stop her sobbing, she explained that when he had left, she took the cubs down to the beach for a midnight run. It was cold and wet. The beach was deserted. The cubs found a discarded boogie-board. Red excitedly insisted that as he was the eldest he should have a go first. He flew up and down the beach skimming across the waves breaking on the beach. They all heard a loud roar as a rogue ninth wave effortlessly picked up Red and the boogie-board and swept them out to sea. It was pitch black. Red had vanished into the night. Terry, Rowan, and Johnny were stunned. They raised their heads and barked and wailed to no avail. They all heard a distant cry for help, then silence. They searched the shore futilely, then despondently, walked slowly back to their den.

When Frank arrived and heard the tragic tale, he shouted out that all might not be lost. He dispatched Rowan to patrol the Middleton side of Eaton Bay and Johnny to race along the Cliff Walk to search for any sign of Red. Ted and Hilda continued searching up and down the beach for the remainder of the night. At dawn Frank let out a shrill bark to call his searchers home. In the safety of their den, he gathered his family in a tight circle and said that he feared that Red had been caught up in a powerful riptide. He might have tried to fight the current, as he was a strong swimmer. He must have become exhausted and drowned. The distraught fox family, exhausted, fell asleep on the floor.

Can you imagine their amazement when they awoke to hear the excited barking of, could they possibly believe it, Red! They raced to the entrance of the den to find Red bedraggled, dripping with water, alive and well. Terry ordered the excited cubs back into the den. It was dawn. People were waking up. Red was dried off with an old beach towel and, after a breakfast of field mice and chestnuts, had recovered sufficiently to tell his tale. He said that as soon as he realized that he was being swept out to sea he abandoned his board. "That was a huge mistake" interjected his worried father, Frank. "Never abandon your ship", he said sternly. Red, ignoring the interruption, continued his tale. "I started swimming back to the lights on shore. It was no use. I was getting tireder and tireder. I thought to myself my goose was cooked. I will never see Rowan, Johnny or my parents again. Suddenly I felt a strong swell of water lifting me up. I thought that the sharks had come for me. To my absolute amazement I realized that it was a dolphin come to rescue me." He said, "My name is Donald." "He lectured me all the way back to the beach." He said, "Never go swimming at night. Never try to swim against a riptide. The tide will always win. Your only chance is to swim sideways away from the current. Out of the riptide you might have a chance of swimming ashore." Donald said that he was getting too old to rescue animals and children swept out to sea. As he deposited me gently on the shore he pointed out the shark fins silhouetted against the light of the early dawn at the entrance to the bay. Red said, "I thanked him profusely and ran straight home, delighted to be back on Terra Firma." Frank said, "Welcome home, son; that was quite a lesson you learned tonight." Frank went on to tell that he had heard at a fox gathering of a similar tale of a drowning sailor being rescued by a dolphin under the Pell Bridge out in Narraganset Bay. Perhaps it was Donald.

# CHAPTER FOUR

# Homeless

The exhausted foxes were dozing around the dining room table when there was a mighty explosion and the roof of their den collapsed. They immediately looked up and were startled to see a spinning wheel protruding through the ceiling. The stunned foxes were instantly mobilized by Frank, barking out "May Day, May Day." The foxes scrambled out the emergency rear exit to the den and hid in the bulrushes around Eaton Pond. Frank and Terry had trained their cubs well. Each den had a muster point. The emergency plan was for each fox to hide in the bulrushes and meet at the old oak tree by the pond at dusk.

Meanwhile, Frank crept down to the beach road to discover the cause of the disaster. He overheard two workmen, from the Department of Roads, discussing the accident. A truck driver had reached down to pick up his cup of Dunkin Donuts coffee from the floor, careened off the road into the bulrushes onto the roof of their den. It took the remainder of the day to tow the truck back onto the road. In the process their den was demolished. Frank thought to himself that losing two dens in two days must be a fox's record.

The five foxes arrived safely at the muster point at dusk. Frank announced that they were going on a camping trip in the country. This was one of the cub's favorite activities. They quickly forgot in their excitement that they had almost been killed that morning and that after losing two dens, that they were homeless. When it was dark, they set off at a brisk pace along the deserted Cliff Walk to Atlantic Drive, then along the rocky seashore to the grounds of the Inn at Castle Hill.

At the entrance to the hotel, there were three beach cottages. Years ago, when Frank was a young cub, he had dug out a den under the deck of Cabin Number 3. He had built the den for just such an emergency. He left Terry and the cubs to clear out the sand and cobwebs. Frank set off to the hotel's kitchen bins. He retrieved three pieces of pizza, half a lobster tail, and a large piece of cod. They all enjoyed a beach picnic at four o'clock in the morning. The cubs promptly fell asleep in the den comfortably lying on the sand with a canvas blanket. Frank and Terry sat up and discussed their next move. Frank stated to his vixen that in the midst of summer, he wasn't really concerned about being homeless. He saw this as a temporary inconvenience. He was much more concerned regarding the growing coyote population on Aquidneck Island.

At the present time the coyotes were hunting solo. They were slipping over the bridges from the mainland. The coyotes were ruthless killers, killing entire flocks of free range chickens just for the sport, not out of hunger. The island foxes were getting the blame. Frank wanted to avoid the local farmers trying to kill the fox population with strychnine- laced meat, leg traps, snares, or aggressive fox hounds. A family of foxes could take on a single coyote, but not a pack of six or seven. Frank told Terry that he had conceived of a plan to rid the island of coyotes. It would involve the cooperation of all the vixens, the ospreys, and the bald eagles. He decided to present his plan at the next foxes' meeting that was held monthly on the night of the full moon. The next meeting was in three days' time.

The foxes met at the Newport StateAirport. They had selected this location as it was in open countryside, in the center of Aquidneck Island. The foxes met at three o'clock in the morning. By this time the islanders were safely home in bed fast asleep. Usually, only the male dog foxes attended the gathering. However, Frank asked Terry to join him for his presentation. They arranged for Ursula, a neighboring vixen who had a den in the woods behind Brenton State Park, to babysit their cubs for the night. Frank and Terry intended to stay the night in an old den overlooking the airport. They had stayed there once before on their honeymoon tour of the island.

# CHAPTER FIVE

# The Foxes Gathering

Three days later, Frank and Terry arrived early for the gathering. They had already swept out their old den and harvested some fresh heather for a bed. There were twenty foxes at the meeting. They had come in from dens all over the island.--from as far north as Island Park, Portsmouth, Middleton, Sachuest Point, Lands End, and Brenton Point. Brian had even swum over from Prudence Island off Coggleshall Point, in Narragansett Bay.

Rufus, the senior fox, called the meeting to order. Frank asked his permission to address the meeting. He began by describing the growing menace of coyotes on the island. They were crossing over the bridges from Bristol, Tiverton, and Jamestown. The rampaging coyotes were killing wildlife, domestic cats, dogs, and hens indiscriminately. Foxes were being blamed. His audience started muttering and growling. If the coyotes were allowed to form packs, the coyotes would quickly hunt down and kill at the foxes, eliminating their only competition for prey.

The audience became very quiet as they contemplated their impending extinction. Having captured his colleagues' attention, Frank went on to explain that he had thought of a possible solution to their dilemma. The foxes were sitting erect and focused on Frank's every word. He proposed asking the ospreys and the bald eagles to perform aerial surveillance of the island coyotes' habitat, and to determine whether they were hunting alone or in packs. Armed with this intelligence, he suggested attacks on the coyotes, at the hour of the wolf, the hour before dawn. He proposed that the ospreys and eagles perform aerial attacks, while the vixens provide their famous blood-curdling cries. Once the terrified coyotes started to run, the dog foxes would

pursue them, driving the coyotes back over the bridges. The night assault, the terrifying vixen cries, the aerial attack of the ospreys and eagles from out of the dark sky, and the pursuit of thirty dog foxes would result in a complete rout of the coyotes. The petrified coyotes would never dream of returning to Aquidneck Island. The entire gathering of foxes rose up on their hind legs and barked out their unanimous support for Frank's bold plan.

# CHAPTER SIX

# Preparations

Rufus asked for a vote on Frank's solution to the coyote population. The foxes voted unanimously to support Frank's plan. He said that the foxes would have to raid the fish market on Long Warf in Newport to obtain enough fresh fish to persuade the ospreys and bald eagles to participate in the hunt.

Rufus thought that the predatory birds would welcome the opportunity to attack the coyotes. These despicable animals had been known to hunt and kill eaglets and osprey chicks-- something that foxes, no matter how hungry they were, would never consider. Once Terry had heard Frank's plan, she spoke up and told the assembled foxes that she would encourage their vixens to join in the vocal assault. The excited foxes dashed back to their dens to spread the news, and all vowed to attend the next gathering.

At the next meeting, Frank was able to report that Ollie, the osprey, leader and Brian, the bald eagle chief, were delighted to participate in the coyote hunt and banishment. However, they both stated that if they spent time tracking, it would reduce their fishing time. Frank had immediately responded that the foxes would supply them with fresh fish for the duration of the mission. The meeting dissolved into an uproar of furious foxes. Dan from Portsmouth shouted out, "How could foxes provide fish for the hunters? We know nothing about fishing." Frank responded, "Well, we are going to have to learn. The birds want lobster, striped bass, salmon, and squid. The ospreys and bald eagles were already out coyote hunting. We had better learn to fish." Liam from the Point in Newport said that squid fishermen stood on the Goat Island bridge jigging their lines with multiple small hooks for squid. Liam said that he had a plank hidden under the bridge. He could easily rescue the occasional squid from the fishing lines as they were reeled in. No one would notice, as the best time to fish for squid was in the dark! Bob, the fox from Thames Street in Newport, said that he knew where the lobstermen on Long Warf stored their lobster until the market price was right. They kept them in metal cages under the pier. He said that he could easily liberate thirty lobsters. Sean, the Navy War College fox, volunteered that there was a salmon fishery off Coddington Point in Narragansett Bay. The fish were in open pens in the water. He said that he would make a raft out of old fishing buoys cast up on the shore. Then he could easily borrow thirty salmon from the pens without being caught.

"And how are we going to catch sea bass?" asked Paddy, the fox from Middleton. Frank immediately responded, "I am going to teach my family to fly fish." His audience was flabbergasted by his reply. So was his vixen, Terry. Rufus suggested that as soon as the fish were caught, they should be delivered to Dyer Island, an uninhabited island out in the bay. The birds would patrol the island every day.

# CHAPTER SEVEN

# Fly Fishing

The previous summer the foxes had watched fly fishermen on Rose Island cast for sea bass. The fly fishermen had discovered a feeding ground for sea bass on the lee side of the island away from all the activity at the lighthouse. Frank and Terry realized that you had to be very patient to catch a sea bass. You had to cast above the feeding fish, and allow the decoy fly to drift down on the current. Once the fish took the fly, the fisherman had ten seconds to set the hook. Then the hard work started, playing the fish. The bass always tried to swim away; you had to let him have plenty of slack line to swim to and fro until he tired. Then you had to slowly reel in the line, keeping the line taut. When the fish was almost on shore, you had to catch him in a net, otherwise he would make a final frantic dash for freedom and escape to live another day. It was a very difficult sport and the beach was littered with abandoned flies, lines, and the occasional sea fly rod, that had been cast into the surf by a frustrated, hungry fisherman.

Over the years, Frank had accumulated a motley array of fly fishing rods, lines, and a vast selection of dry flies. He had squirreled away this collection in his den among the rocks for just such an occasion.

Frank and Terry had evacuated their den at Castle Hill and led Red, Rowan, and Johnny down the length of Thames Street to the Pell Bridge. Then they quietly swam out to Rose Island at four o'clock in the morning. The cubs were very excited. Frank pilfered three lobsters from the traps under the bridge. No easy maneuver. His paws were pinched several times while rescuing the lobsters from the kitchen and parlours of the lobster traps. Then he had to knock out the lobsters with a heavy rock, tie them together, and then tow them back to the den for breakfast. He was utterly exhausted. Terry and the cubs were extremely impressed and allowed him to enjoy an entire lobster tail himself. They spent the rest of the day dozing in their warm den.

Once it was dusk, it was time to start fishing. Each cub had his own rod. Frank and Terry set it up as a fishing competition. Each cub was responsible for choosing their own flies, tying them to the line, and then casting the fly out onto the ocean. Rowan caught the first sea bass, hooked by his tail. Johnny and Red rolled around the beach roaring with laughter. They almost lost their rods in the excitement. Once they settled down, they steadily reeled them in. They became a fly fishing team: Red casting and landing the fish, Rowan using a discarded net to catch the fish, and Johnny dispatching the fish with a heavy rock on the head. They stored the sea bass in the larder in their den. They feasted on sea bass and then collapsed into an exhausted sleep. Frank and Terry sat up for a little while and discussed their next problem. They had to transport twenty large sea bass five miles up Narragansett Bay against the tide and the current to Dyer Island. They decided to sleep on the problem.

That evening Terry sat up out of a restful sleep. She said the solution is obvious. Ospreys and eagles can fly and carry their prey. She immediately dispatched Frank along the shore road to Dyer Island. She told him to inform the birds that their fish awaited them on Rose Island. The cubs were amazed to see their father return to them by air. He was carried in the talons of two bald eagles. The sea bass were accepted and the quest for coyotes started in earnest. The foxes' scouts discovered a pack of five coyotes living in Island Park just over the bridge from Tiverton. There were another three lone coyotes scattered across the island, two in Sachuset Point National Wildlife refuge, and one in FortAdams State Park. At the next foxes' meeting, they decided to form two teams. Frank's family with their bald eagle friends, Brian and Sophie, would rout out the Sachuset Point coyotes. The remainder of the island foxes and the ospreys would surround the Island Park coyotes and drive them over the Tiverton Bridge.

The plan went like clockwork. The Island Park coyotes were rudely awakened to the vixen's blood-curdling screeches and were then viciously attacked by aerial assault by the ospreys. The island foxes drove them to the Tiverton bridge. The terrified coyotes shot across never to return.

At the southeast corner of the island, Frank's family drove the two coyotes down to Third Beach and onto an old wooden rowing boat. The bald eagles then towed the boat across the Sakonnet River and released them on the Little Compton Shore. The foxes decided to leave the lone old coyote in Adams State Park in peace. They knew if he caused any trouble, they could take care of him.

# CHAPTER EIGHT

# Country Pursuits

Frank decided that it was time to bring his cubs out into the country in order to teach them how to hunt for their breakfast. In the city, they had always relied on "take away food" from the restaurants. Red, Rowan and Johnny hadn't a clue how to hunt for fresh meat.

One clear moonlit night in July, Frank led his family away from the bright lights of Newport, out past the Newport vineyards into the open countryside. Frank and Terry first taught the cubs how to build a bivouac. Frank always traveled with a four foot square piece of canvas, rescued from the dumpster outside a sail-maker's loft on Thames Street. He showed them how to anchor the top of the tent with rocks along a stone wall, then to stretch the canvas out until it was taut. He then deposited a series of rocks along the base. *Viola*! A bivouac! He then showed them how to camouflage the camp with a few branches from the local trees. It was now invisible. He then led them out into the adjacent cornfield. Frank, Terry and the cubs lined up along each side of the field, then, noisily started forward. The field mice retreated and were slowly driven into the center of the field. At a critical moment, the mice suddenly realized their predicament and made a dash for freedom. Chaos ensued as the foxes chased the terrified mice and pounced. Johnny, being the youngest was given the responsibility of bringing the dead mice back to camp, while the others hunted on.

# CHAPTER NINE

# Rabbit Hunting

Frank was delighted with his team of mice-hunters. The following evening, they moved their camp to the wind generators on the hills overlooking Portsmouth Abbey School. The gentle rolling hills had become a rabbit warren. The local conservationists felt that the rabbits had been attracted by the soft sounds of the spinning wind turbines. Frank and Terry knew the best time to catch a rabbit was at dawn or dusk when they were out quietly grazing. They decided on a strategy of taking most advantage of the five foxes. They lay prone in the thick grass around the rabbit holes and silently waited for the dawn. At first light the unsuspecting rabbits sauntered out and started nibbling the grass.

Frank had instructed his family not to move until twenty rabbits were out in the open. When they heard their father's bark, the cubs were instructed to run to the nearest burrow and block the entrance. The rabbits panicked, confused and disoriented by the blocked burrows. Frank and Terry raced around dispatching the bunnies. Within three minutes they had five rabbits to bring home.

That morning the foxes dined on a fresh bunny and buried the remainder deep in the soil as a larder for their next trip to the area. Life was good.

# CHAPTER TEN

# Wild Turkey Hunting

From an early age, Frank and Terry had taught their cubs to climb trees. It was an essential fox skill. They could escape predators like coyotes, heaven forbid, by climbing. Frank decided to teach his family a trick that he had learned from his father, how to catch a wild turkey. It was well known to foxes that wild turkeys were notoriously difficult to catch. They had excellent eyesight and remarkable hearing. If they thought they were in danger these cumbersome birds had the strength to fly straight up in the air like Harrier Jump Jets, and perch safely in the trees. After years of study and contemplation, Frank's father had devised an incredibly dangerous way to catch a wild turkey. It was worth the challenge as wild turkeys were as delicious as the famous Scottish bird, Haggis.

Frank dispatched Rowan and Johnny to hunt through the fields until they found a flock of wild turkeys. Then he instructed them to shadow the turkeys until they flew up into the trees to roost at dusk. The following day Frank had Red, his eldest and strongest cub, climb high up into the turkeys tree, wedge himself into a crevice between a branch and the trunk, and wait. Once the turkeys had returned and dozed off to sleep, he was instructed to quietly stretch out and pounce on the back of a dormant turkey and hold on for dear life. The panicked bird would resort to instinct and glide down through the trees to land quietly in the woods. Then the family would attack and quickly dispatch the terrified turkey.

"Great plans of mice and men often go awry," Robbie Burns. Initially the plan went like clockwork. The distraught turkey tried to buck Red off his back. It was an impossible task to

attempt while trying to fly. Then the turkey tried to brush Red off his back by flying through a very narrow gap between two trees. Red, bruised and battered, held on. Finally, when the turkey landed, he spun Red off his back and started aggressively attacking his assailant.

In the nick of time, Red's family arrived like the cavalry. Frank went for the jugular and the battle was over. The jubilant foxes dragged the wild turkey home to their camp and feasted all night. What an adventure. Red was the hero of the hour.

# CHAPTER ELEVEN

# The Den

When all the cubs had fallen into an exhausted sleep, Frank and Terry stayed up and gazed at the moon. Terry told Frank it was time he built a new den for her. Winter was coming and she expected a new litter of cubs in the Spring. Frank hugged her and asked her whether she liked camels. She said that that was the most ridiculous question she had ever been asked. She responded, "Are you crazy?" Frank, with a wide grin on his face said that he had given the idea of a new den considerable thought. He had decided on building a town den and a country den. Now Terry knew he was crazy. He rapidly explained that he was going to build her a den at Doris Duke's house, "Rough Point", on BellevueAvenue, overlooking the ocean. Doris was a multimillionaire. She had once bought a personal jet from a SaudiArabian prince. Two camels were included in the sale. Doris decided to keep the two camels, Princess and Baby, with her in the summer in Newport and transport them back to her New Jersey estate to keep them in her heated stables for the winter. Her estate was now a museum, open during the day, locked up at night. There was no one living in her house to disturb the foxes. The camels were now living in luxury in a New Jersey Zoo. However, they had left behind an enormous pile of dung. Frank told Terry he would bring the cubs to Rough Point and build his masterpiece, a den carved out of camel dung. Terry was amazed. She had thought that Frank only lived in the moment, and had never given any thought to the future. She was impressed. She said, "Where are you thinking of for our country den. He immediately replied, "Sachuset Point National Wildlife Reservation." The following night the entire family went to explore. Rowan found a perfect location amidst the rushes. The ground was level and firm. There was a magnificent view of St. George's School up on the hill. This was a phenomenal source for scavenging. They were also close to the beach.

The foxes set to work digging a den. They dug all night, then collapsed into an exhausted sleep. Red was first up the following evening. He went outside for a quick pee. He rushed back, sounding the alarm. The entire den, front and back entrances were surrounded by a circle of two hundred irate animals. The sleepy foxes roused out of a deep sleep were shocked and appalled.

Frank and Terry had thought that their family would have been welcomed into the sanctuary for driving the coyotes out of the reserve.

An enormousArctic owl, Owen, addressed the terrified foxes. He exclaimed, "Foxes are not welcome here. You live by hunting and eating wildlife. None of us will be safe with foxes in the reserve; friends one night, dinner the next. This cannot be tolerated. We would however like to thank you for ridding the reservation of the unscrupulous coyotes." That admission gave Frank a glimmer of hope. Perhaps they could reach a compromise. He said that his family were vegetarians and planned to live on wild berries, mushrooms and tomatoes from gardens outside the reservation.

Owen and the animals looked at the foxes in amazement. Owen repeated incredulously, "Vegetarian foxes?" "Yes," said Frank. "Well semi-veg." Owen repeated, "Semi-veg? "Yes," said Frank. "We also like to fly fish for sea bass off the beach." Now all the animals and his family gazed at him stunned into silence. Owen finally broke the silence by saying, "This is most unexpected." He said that he would have to consult with his colleagues. They immediately went into a noisy huddle. The animals were divided in their opinion as whether to trust this family of "semi-veg" foxes. After twenty minutes of lively debate, the Arctic owl proposed a compromise. The foxes could stay if they behaved. They were banned from hunting or bringing dead animals into the reserve to eat. They could fish. All the animals looked forward to watching them fly fish. Any infringement of these rules, the foxes would be out of the reserve for life and their den destroyed. Frank immediately agreed and shook Owen's enormous wing with his right paw. "Deal," he said.

# CHAPTER TWELVE

# Rough Point

When the stunned foxes returned to their dens, after the circle of animals had dispensed, Frank said "Well, that was interesting. We now have a country home. Tomorrow, we will slip into Newport at dusk along the Cliff Walk to start creating our new winter den." They had a late night swim at Rejects Beach, then they started surveying the camel dung heap beside the stables. It was eight feet tall and mounded like the hump on a camel. Over the years the moisture had evaporated and the residue was firm and odorless. Frank decided to start digging on the stable side of the heap, away from prying eyes. As they dug, Frank instructed his cubs to scatter the hard clay around the gardens. Red, Rowan and Johnny used to disappear into the moonlight starring at the topiary, green trees and shrubs that had been shaped by pruning into exotic animals. At Rough Point there were two topiary camels standing seven feet tall, modeled on two live camels that lived in the gardens from June to September, Princess and Baby. These were camels with two humps from CentralAsia. The cubs loved the exotic gardens. Frank decided that their den, nestled among the Newport mansions, would be a masterpiece. He decided to create a tunnel from one side to the other. Then he had the cubs hollow out the center of the dung heap with two bedrooms off the central dining room. He then had the cubs scour the cliff walk and beaches to search for flotsam, as opposed to jetsam. The difference in nautical terms is concise. Flotsam is washed off a ship by breaking waves. Jetsam is an object discarded intentionally from a ship. He had then searched for planks and old lobster traps. He used the planks as wainscoting on the front and back entrances. Then he had them haul two traps into the dining room of the den. Finally, the entire family lifted two planks onto the two traps that were standing upright to support the ceiling. Frank and Terry sent the cubs to collect boughs of heather from the Newport Golf Club. They placed the heather on the floor of the two bedrooms. Red found two large wooden croquet balls in the flower beds behind the mansion. They used these balls to block the entrances from the inside to keep out drafts and intruders. The wall in their dining room was decorated with fishing rods, toy boats and shovels, all found discarded on the beach. Terry was delighted with the plank dining table and the root cellar for storing potatoes, carrots, and apples for the winter.

G. D'Arcy '21

## CHAPTER THIRTEEN

# The Ghost Hunt

Every year on March fifth, the feast day of St. Kieran, the patron saint of foxes, Frank and Terry brought their cubs to a hill near the Newport Polo Club to see the ghost hunt. When they arrived on the hillside, overlooking the Polo ground fields, it was packed with boisterous foxes. At two o'clock in the morning, they heard the distant sound of horns. They saw a fleeing fox shimmering in the moonlight. As he fled past the foxes mesmerized on the hill, he winked and waved his paw. This ghostly apparition was followed in hot pursuit by a pale white pack of baying hounds, finally a silent troop of huntsmen mounted on their ghostly horses, racing after the shimmering hounds. Then quiet descended on the hill until the foxes heard the distant bark of Rex, the red fox, announcing that all was well. When the foxes had safely returned to their den in the sanctuary, Frank told the cubs that the origin of the ghostly hunt had taken place a hundred years earlier.

Red, the fox, had led the pack of ferocious hounds to the cliffs at Castle Hill. Red was the first over the cliff. He immediately dropped down three feet onto a narrow ledge. The hounds and the huntsmen shot over the cliff and plunged down eighty feet and perished in the ocean. Red was the only one to survive. The ghostly hunt reappears once a year on St. Kieran's Day.

# CHAPTER FOURTEEN

# A Surfeit of Skunks

One bright evening Frank and Terry were relaxing outside their palatial den at Rough Point, enjoying the sunshine. All the visitors to the estate had long departed. They were sharing a dish of freshly squeezed apple juice, when Frank's cousin, Eddy, strolled into the garden. Frank hid his surprise and welcomed Eddy. He lived on Jamestown Island. He must have slipped over the two mile Pell Bridge during the night. It was a risky trip. After quenching his thirst with apple juice, Eddy got straight to the point of his mission. He said, "Jamestown was in an uproar. The skunk population had exploded. The skunks had become very bold." They were invading the restaurants on NarragansettAvenue during dinner on the outdoor patios. They were climbing the trellis fences and meandering among the diners, terrifying them. The restaurateurs were taking drastic action to cull the skunk population. They were leaving out tasty morsels of food laced with strychnine. Skunks and fox cubs were dying at an alarming rate. The Jamestown Sportsman's Club was organizing a skunk hunt that weekend. Something had to be done to save the skunk and fox population of Jamestown. Frank asked Eddy, "Why did you come to me?" Eddy responded, "You are famous for ridding Aquidneck Island of coyotes. You are known to be very resourceful. If you decide to travel to Jamestown to help us, we will be happy to replenish your root cellar with carrots, potatoes, brussels sprouts and apples for the winter." Frank replied, "We were thinking of a summer holiday on Jamestown Island and will be happy to try and solve your dilemma." Terry never came across a problem she didn't like. Frank and

Terry agreed that the coyote solution wouldn't work. They were going to have to come up with another solution. If they could lure the skunks off the island their problem would be solved.

Frank went off to consult his friend, Sammy the Skunk, from Spring Street. Sammy lived with his family under one of the old porches. He had often dined with Frank and his family on the food remnants in the dumpsters behind the restaurants on Thames Street. Frank asked Sammy, "What are skunks' favorite foods?" Sammy immediately replied, "Acorns." Frank recalled that from his travels as a young cub, that there was a forest of oak trees around the University of Rhode Island in Kingston. There was also an agriculture college with a model farm and a market garden. Frank put Terry in charge of their cubs and sent them out to collect as many acorns as possible in supermarket plastic bags. He sent Eddy back to Jamestown to invite the island population of skunks to a crisis meeting the following night on the second green at Jamestown Golf Course at two o'clock in the morning. That night Frank's family with five bags of acorns crept over the Pell bridge to Jamestown, keeping in the shadows. When they arrived at Eddy's den at five o'clock in the morning, beside the third fairway in the rushes, Eddy had prepared a feast of mushrooms, clams, potatoes and field mice.

At the meeting with the skunks Frank outlined his dismay with the persecution of the innocent animals. He told them of the wonderful oak forest in Kingston, the fields of carrots, lettuces, peas and sweet corn at the agricultural college. He then went on to describe the fantastic amounts of food discarded by the college students. He said that he would be happy to guide them over the Verranzo Bridge to these Elysian Fields. He told them that it was critical for the skunks to leave the island for good, as the natives were organizing weekly hunts until all the skunks were exterminated. It was time to leave. A strange procession of muddy wet skunks set off the following night. Frank had them roll in the mud and soak their fur to disguise their white hair. The cubs led the way strewing the side of the road with delicious acorns. When the weary travelers arrived at the college they were delighted with the abundance of scrumptious food. They all thanked Frank, Terry and Eddy profusely, and vowed never to return to the dangerous island of Jamestown.

# CHAPTER FIFTEEN

# The Newport to Bermuda Race

At dusk the entire family went to see the sailors preparing for the Newport to Bermuda race, across six hundred miles of open ocean. They went down to the Newport Boat Yard. All the sailors were busy stocking the boats and checking their rigging. Johnny climbed on board one yacht on the dock for a closer look and peered through the open forward skyhatch, where they stored the sails in bags. Johnny took a closer look and toppled over into the cockpit. He was trapped. The walls were sheer. His family were amazed at the sudden turn of events. It started to rain and the sailors raced around and closed all the hatches. Johnny was going to Bermuda!

He laid low like a stowaway. He emerged from the sail storage cabin when they were far out to sea with two dead mice in his paws. He dropped them at the feet of the yacht's captain who was sitting at the navigation station in the saloon. He looked up and stared at Johnny. He said, "I see we have a stowaway." "You will have to earn your keep, catching mice, swabbing the decks and keeping the crew at the helm awake during the night watches." Johnny immediately became the yacht's mascot and the sailors fed him scraps from their plates. He discovered that with four paws he was very stable on the boat as it raced through the ocean. He was mesmerized by the pods of dolphins that cavorted in the bow waves. He wondered if one of them had rescued Red when he had been washed out to sea on his boogie-board. Once they sailed across the Gulf Stream, Johnny was in charge of removing the flying fish from the decks each morning. They were his favorite snack. Two hundred miles from Bermuda, he was swabbing the deck at dawn, when a thirty foot minke whale shot completely out of the ocean, straight up in the air. Its entire body was visible, and then he dived and disappeared. Johnny thought that the whale was curious and decided to have a look at this strange whale sailing past him.

When the yacht sailed past St. David's light at two o'clock in the morning, the race was over. They docked at the marina in Hamilton. Johnny was first on shore. He raced along the shore road, as far as the National Museum of Bermuda, in the fort of the Royal Naval Dockyard. On the Port's ramparts, reclining on the grass in the warm sunshine, he spotted the most glamorous gray fox vixen he had ever seen. The reader has to realize that Johnny had been at sea for over three days. It was love at first sight. Her name was Raquel. She was anxious to travel and see the world. Four days later Raquel and a rather sheepish Johnny stepped on board the yacht for the return trip to Bermuda. Captain David and his crew teased Johnny all the way home. They told Raquel that Johnny had a vixen in every port. They told Johnny that he was a very fast mover for a fox. When they disembarked in Newport, Johnny had matured into a cosmopolitan fox. He took Raquel on a tour of the island, and they decided to establish a den overlooking the cliffs at Castle Hill. The den had a spectacular view overlooking Brenton Reef, the start of the Newport to Bermuda Race.

## CHAPTER SIXTEEN

# Full Circle

Frank was basking in the afternoon sunshine outside his winter den at Rough Point. His two cubs, Red and Rowan, were fast asleep beside him. Terry approached him and said, "I am expecting another litter of cubs in the spring. It is time that Red and Rowan left the den and started their own families. Frank was delighted with the news and shocked by the fact that his babies were old enough to start their own families.

Frank broached the subject of leaving home over breakfast with Red and Rowan. Red leapt at the opportunity to leave. He didn't like sharing a bedroom anymore. He had an adorable vixen in mind and was anxious to establish his own den. Red had already chosen a site at St. George's School. He had found a den site on the steep bank below the school with a majestic view of Long Island Sound.

Rowan said that he had thoroughly enjoyed his childhood and adolescence with his parents. He had no particular vixen in mind. He wanted to play the field before deciding. He was also anxious to establish his own den. Rowan wanted to live on Jamestown Island. When they were removing the skunks, he had found a potential den overlooking Mackerel Cove. The den was adjacent to the beach and a rabbit warren. Rowan also was keen to leave his parents den before the new cubs arrived. The noise and disruption would ruin his pursuit of a beautiful vixen. When Johnny and Raquel arrived, the entire family settled down to enjoy a seafood brunch.

Frank and Terry were delighted that their cubs were planning to stay in the area. They were looking forward to seeing their grandchildren and how Red, Rowan, and Johnny would handle their cubs. It would be an interesting year!

Printed in the United States
by Baker & Taylor Publisher Services